Mis deportes favoritos / My Favorite Sports

ME ENCANTA EL FÚTBOL AMERICANO/ I LOVE FOOTBALL

By Ryan Nagelhout

Traducido por Eida de la Vega

Gareth Stevens PUBLISHING

Please visit our website, www.garethstevens.com. For a free color catalog of all our high-quality books, call toll free 1-800-542-2595 or fax 1-877-542-2596.

Library of Congress Cataloging-in-Publication Data

Nagelhout, Ryan.
I love football = Me encanta el fútbol americano / by Ryan Nagelhout.
p. cm. — (My favorite sports = Mis deportes favoritos)
Parallel title: Mis deportes favoritos
In English and Spanish.
Includes index.
ISBN 978-1-4824-0850-8 (library binding)
1. Football — Juvenile literature. I. Nagelhout, Ryan. II. Title.
GV950.7 N34 2015
796.332—d23

First Edition

Published in 2015 by
Gareth Stevens Publishing
111 East 14th Street, Suite 349
New York, NY 10003

Editor: Ryan Nagelhout
Designer: Nick Domiano
Spanish Translation: Eida de la Vega

Photo credits: Cover, pp.1 (football player), 5, 9, 24 (helmet) Monkey Business Images/Shutterstock.com; cover, p.1 (background) majeczka/Shutterstock.com; pp. 7, 17 Andrew Rich/Vetta/Getty Images; p. 11 Bill Grove/E+/Getty Images; pp. 13, 15 Amy Myers/Shutterstock.com; pp. 19, 24 (end zone) SAJE/Shutterstock.com; p. 21 Stockbyte/Thinkstock.com; p. 23 Yellow Dog Productions/The Image Bank/Getty Images.

Printed in the United States of America

CPSIA compliance information: Batch #CS15GS: For further information contact Gareth Stevens, New York, New York at 1-800-542-2595.

Contenido

Contents

¡Me encanta jugar fútbol americano!

I love to play football!

Juego con mis amigos.

I play it with my friends.

20
16
32
47
3

Uso un casco.
Me protege la cabeza.

I wear a football helmet.
It keeps my head safe.

Mi amigo me
lanza la pelota.

My friend throws me
the ball.

A él le gusta ser mariscal de campo.

He likes to play quarterback.

Me gusta ser corredor.

I like to play
running back.

Corro muy rápido
con la pelota.

I run the ball really fast.

Corro hasta el final
del terreno. Se llama la
zona de anotación.

I run to the end of the
field. This is called the
end zone.

¡Me encanta anotar!

I love to score touchdowns!

¡Ven a jugar
fútbol conmigo!

Come play football
with me!

Palabras que debes saber/ Words to Know

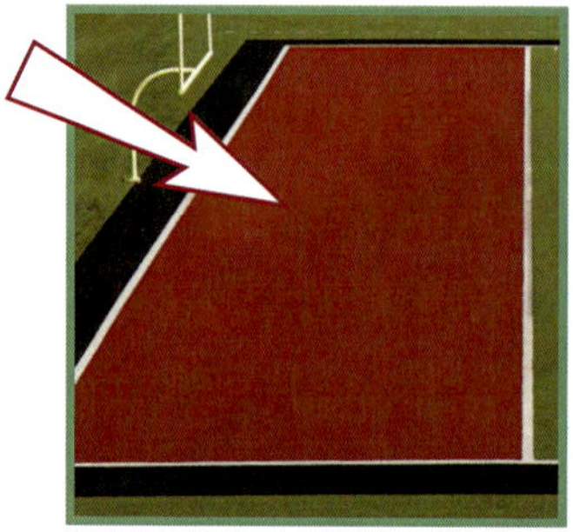

la zona de anotación/ end zone

el casco/ helmet

Índice / Index